Adeline

Happy Reading

Cassandra M. Carnaher

Adeline

A NOVEL BY

Cassandra Carraher

Book design by The Troy Book Makers

Printed in the United States of America

The Troy Book Makers • Troy, New York • thetroybookmakers.com

To order additional copies of this title, contact your favorite local bookstore or visit www.shoptbmbooks.com

ISBN: 978-1-61468-434-3

Dedicated to my family, friends,
and Girl Scout Troop 2304, as
well as everyone who has helped me
throughout my journey...especially
Mr. DeBiase, my English teacher.

And It Began

Adeline was born in 1901, with shoulder length brown hair, natural blonde streaks, and green eyes. Now eleven, Adeline continued to become even more curious about her unknown past. She lived in an all girls' orphanage in Savannah, Georgia. The orphanage was made out of red brick and the girls' beds were lined up in two rows across the walls on the inside. There was a boys' orphanage across the street, which none of the girls were allowed to enter. It was only a little way away, but it felt like it was an eternity away. Near the boys' orphanage were shops and other houses. It always seemed more lively than the girls' orphanage.

The only belonging that Adeline had of her own was a mirror. The mirror had a green, jade handle and a silver frame. On its back was a design of flowers, also made from the same silver of the frame. She also had a blue dress, though she wouldn't call it her own. The dress had a white collar and a green ribbon. She had "borrowed" that ribbon from a girl that had found a home. However, the collar she had sewn on herself. After all, Adeline was trained to be a maid, cook assistant, and a seamstress during her time at the orphanage. She dreamed of one day getting a decent job and using the money she earned to uncover her past, perhaps she would even find her parents.

Today was Adeline's birthday. It wasn't her "real" birthday though. It was only the day at the orphanage when they celebrated everyone's birthdays because many didn't know their real ones. Adeline had lived at the orphanage all of her life so she had come to peace with the idea of a shared birthday. When she had arrived at the orphanage as a newborn, she was covered in lace. She clutched the mirror in her hand with no other explanation. The lace had surely been used to make clothing for the other girls, so her mirror was her prized possession. They had let her keep it; they hadn't sold it. That was a small mercy.

Adeline was a daydreamer, but she could get her work done faster than most. She said that it was because she could imagine what would happen if she didn't. She followed the rules, but often found herself about to break them. Adeline wasn't a troublemaker, but she wasn't a proper lady like her friend Jane.

Jane was the one who was always able to inspire all the girls at the orphanage. Jane was Adeline's only good friend. Jane even had a surname! Her full name was Jane Violet Gothum. Adeline admired Jane's identity, yet yearned to find her own, too.

Jane had curly, strawberry blonde hair and good intelligence. All of the boys loved her, so Adeline was mostly hidden in her shadow. Adeline sometimes envied Jane, but the feeling quickly disappeared when she saw how much Jane trusted her. Jane told Adeline all her secrets, and Adeline, Jane. Though how many secrets could two orphan girls have? Adeline never told any of the other girls Jane's secrets of course!

Adeline was a favorite in the schoolroom. That was one thing she had going for herself over Jane. It wasn't because Adeline was smarter than Jane, it was only because Adeline didn't ask stupid or impossible questions aloud. Instead, she just pondered them to herself.

Adeline didn't like any boys since no one was really supposed to like boys. However, most girls did. They were only able to see the boys in church and on Fridays because on Fridays the boys would always play sports on their front lawn. That was when the girls would all rush to the window, just to see their favorite score a goal, to later get lectured, and do it again next Friday.

Adeline now waited in line for the washroom with Jane getting impatient next to her. She looked at Jane and then at the other girls waiting. Half an hour later, or so it seemed, it was their turn. The girls went in pairs to try and speed things up, but it didn't help. After they were done, Jane skipped to her bed which was across the wall from Adeline's. Adeline undid her hair and let it fall. Jane did the same with her shoulder-length hair. All of the girls at the orphanage kept their hair at the same length to look similar.

It was a cool night that was the perfect temperature. "Best night of the year," Jane muttered as her eyes closed. Adeline agreed, but for a strange reason couldn't fall asleep. She felt as though it was too perfect and turned to face Jane. Staring at the girl who looked so peaceful lured Adeline to sleep.

Jane daintily tapped Adeline's shoulder and woke Adeline up from the middle of a dream. In the dream Adeline had been finding a mermaid at sea. It was still dark and about two or three in the morning. Jane looked worried, which was unusual for her. She sat on Adeline's bed and slowly told in a small sleepy voice that she couldn't sleep.

Adeline sighed and sat up. She began to sing a lullaby that seemed to echo through the silent town. It was whimsical and pure. Jane yawned and urged her to keep singing. Whenever there was a storm or something unsettling Adeline would sing to the orphan girls. They eventually all fell asleep and it was silent again. Adeline's voice was a secret kept for her and the orphan girls. It was the only thing that she could truly call her own talent.

* * *

Adeline quickly washed her face and got dressed. She had slept late and a visitor was coming today. Adeline pulled a string out of her dress and used it to tie up her hair. She tried to look as responsible and polite as she could. She daydreamed through her work until around lunchtime. When she had a break Adeline put down her sewing, stabbing herself with the needle in the process, and walked over to the cluster of girls forming.

They were waiting for the visitor just as they heard a knock on the door. The lady at the door was wearing a grey dress with lace trimming. It made her look regal in a dark manner. She told Miss Blake, their teacher, some information. She whispered in a ladylike voice that she needed a maid for the Low household. Miss Blake nodded and brought Jane, Adeline, and Rebecca to her office. Rebecca was rude and slacked sometimes, so Adeline thought that she had a chance against her. Adeline would never have a chance against Jane, but that didn't stop her from standing tall and doing her best impersonation of a responsible person.

Miss Blake told how each of the girls worked and how fast they did it. Jane squeezed Adeline's hand behind their backs and that made them both smile. The lady asked how they felt towards boys and Miss Blake hesitated out of surprise. Ladies weren't supposed to talk of these matters.

Miss Blake glanced at the girls and, with some hesitation, told them to speak. Rebecca was honest and said that she liked them, when Jane said that they liked her. Adeline was bold and said that they underestimated her. The women smiled happily and told Miss Blake that Adeline was the girl that she was looking for.

* * *

Everyone congratulated Adeline as she walked out the door. She wore a bonnet of her own and a Rosary tucked in her dress pocket, along with her mirror. She walked behind the lady, who was named Miss Nash. It was early in morning, people were trickling into the streets and shops were opening. Miss Nash led her to a part of town that she had never been to before. It was richer, with only rows of houses and no shops. They walked down a cobblestone path, with trees lining the way. It directed them to a house.

Adeline put her hands in her pockets and stroked her mirror. Miss Nash quickly recited the standard speech that she gave all the workers. The speech informed Adeline of her duties and what not to do, however it didn't mention anything about the household. The house itself was on the corner of the street and painted a cream color. It's shutters were brown, and brick stairs connected from the doorway to the both sides of the house. One right and one left. To the right of the entrance was a grey colored deck with white pillars and fencing. From the entrance hung a flag on an aged, metal pole. Around the house were blooming flower bushes with reddish-pinkish flowers. Underneath the main entrance was a small wooden door hidden between the stairs and covered in metal gates. Miss Nash opened that door to a long hallway that was brightly lit as she remarked to Adeline, "Welcome!"

Warm Welcome

Miss Nash quickly slid through a small paneled door that was not easily visible from the grand hallway. She told Adeline in a superior voice that the staircase going up leads to the servant's quarters, and the stairs going down lead to the kitchen. Miss Nash commanded, "Go to your room and then meet the others in the kitchen. Your room number is two."

Adeline eagerly walked up the old wooden stairs to her room. They creaked with each step. She finally reached the top and quickly found the wooden door with the rusted "2" on it.

The room was painted white, and small yet cozy. There was a bowl filled with water on a shelf, for washing, along with a small, wooden bed frame covered with a scratchy wool blanket and small feather pillow. Adeline placed her extra clothes on this bed and put her Rosary on a small shelf above the washing bowl. Her bonnet went alongside her Rosary. Adeline pushed a strand of her hair that had escaped her bun behind her ear and scurried quickly down the stairs to the kitchen.

Adeline was joyfully greeted at the door by Miss Smith who was a short, older woman. The other servants and Miss Nash sat at the table drinking tea. Miss Nash stood up and introduced Adeline in the same superior voice that she had before. Miss Smith went to fetch some tea for Adeline, her brown hair tied in a loose braid with strains flying out here and there.

Next, Miss Nash introduced Rosemary, the cook's assistant who was a shy older girl with black wavy hair. The other maid, Vivian, welcomed Adeline to the open chair next to her. As Adeline settled into her seat Miss Smith handed her a cup of warm tea. Samuel, an old pinched-nose page boy, sat across. He was going to be replaced soon. Vivian reminded Adeline of Jane, in an odd way. They looked similar with the same jawline and facial features. The only difference was that Vivian's hair was a dark, red velvet color and Vivian was a year or two older than Jane.

Vivian sipped the rest of her tea and brought the empty teacup to the counter next to the sink. Adeline did the same when she was done. Miss Nash then handed Adeline a list of chores to do. They were written on a yellowing piece of paper and were labeled by day and time. As Adeline reviewed the sheet, Miss Nash handed her another aging document. This one was a handwritten map of the house. Samuel called after Adeline as she left. "You'll get used to it," Samuel insisted in a wise guy voice.

Adeline opened the paneled door and stood in the hallway. Now for the first task of polishing the silverware, Adeline walked to the dining room. There was a fireplace with a big gold mirror hanging above it, along with a long, wooden table that had chairs with velvet green cushions. The floor was patterned with a red and green rug. A gold chandelier hung above it all with four snowball shaped light bulbs. There were two windows along the wall, with green and white curtains. In the room, on the opposite wall from the fireplace, was a brown, wooden cupboard. It held all of the silverware and plates. Adeline polished each piece until she could see herself in every single one, and then dusted off the cupboard itself.

* * *

The list of chores eventually grew shorter and so did the day. Adeline had one more thing to do before supper. She skimmed over the nearly paragraph-long-list of chore descriptions. It turned out to not be as detailed as you would expect. It explained that Adeline must go to the market, if it wasn't already closed, and buy some items. Executing this task included getting money from Miss Nash, fetching a basket from the kitchen, and finding a map of the neighborhood. She had to buy cologne and some pearls, which she assumed were for someone in the Low family. Adeline already knew that the servants would never see these luxuries again after she delivered them to Miss Nash. This was expected by the servants, and Adeline took pleasure in the task of shopping.

* * *

After getting all the supplies that Adeline required, she headed to the market. She wanted to get everything that she needed before it closed. Adeline picked a cologne that smelled like fresh flowers and was colored like pink pearls. Breaking even with no change, she arrived back at the kitchen right when everyone was sitting down to eat. She gave her goods to Miss Nash, then hustled to her seat.

Supper today was soup and more tea. The soup was more of a watered-down chili, surely leftovers. Even so, it was better than anything at the orphanage and Adeline quickly finished off two bowls. Vivian grinned, and Miss Nash nodded approvingly, thinking that at least someone appreciated the food. Samuel ignored Miss Nash's achievement and kept on eating.

After the meal, Adeline dreamily wandered off to her room. Her stomach nearly exploded from eating so much food. Until now, she had never truly known how it felt to be full. She washed her face and looked in her mirror. Then, she tore her eyes away and read a little bit of the Bible, saying her prayers. When she fell asleep she dreamed of dancing on the sun while she lay cold in bed.

3

A Boy and A Vest

Adeline had been working for a week now and it was time for Samuel to leave. Adeline was abruptly awakened by Vivian at 6:00 and, as per the usual, quickly got ready. Today for breakfast they had buttered toast with plain water. Samuel ate more voraciously this morning, wanting to make the most of the day. To Adeline, he was just another sloppy boy, and always would be. Samuel's replacement would come at dinner time. Adeline and Vivian hoped that it was someone more becoming.

Today's chores seemed to take days, but finally Adeline finished. She headed to supper hoping for some more of that watery chili stuff. She walked into the kitchen door and stopped dead in her tracks. Miss Nash was talking to a tall boy, who was a couple of years older than Adeline. Adeline could only see his back from her viewpoint. The only person that seemed to notice her entering the room was Rosemary. Rosemary was sitting on a stool trying to hide a smile by cutting fresh carrots.

Adeline returned her focus to the boy and studied him from a better area of the kitchen. His hair was a golden sunshine color and his eyes were green, dotted with brown specks. Miss Nash was giving the boy the same lecture that Adeline had received, give or take some parts. The boy seemed to be listening, but his hands were fiddling with something in his pocket. Adeline smiled at this image, remembering fondly that she, too, had acted the same way. She had been touching her prized mirror. The memory still lingered now.

Miss Nash swiftly turned towards Adeline, knocking her out of her dream land. Then she introduced Adeline and the boy in a tired voice, which Adeline hadn't noticed before. The boy's name was Byron. He smiled at her and she smiled back. Rosemary giggled in the background.

"This is Rosemary," Miss Nash said, clearly annoyed. Rosemary continued to giggle and was now overcome with the hiccups, nearly cutting off a finger in her carrot cutting expedition.

"Careful," Miss Nash warned, before handing out the schedules for tomorrow. Vivian bounced down the stairs and was the next to be introduced.

Adeline sat down with Vivian at her right and Byron at her left. Rosemary was across from Adeline, with Miss Smith and Miss Nash at the heads of the table. They sat and ate their water chili with a side of rock hard bread. They drank their nightly tea and were shipped off to their rooms. Byron received room eight. The girls had rooms 1-5 and the boys had 6-10. Adeline followed her same nightly routine before retiring to her bed. A boy had never affected her so much.

* * *

Adeline awoke to Vivian who was standing in the doorway tapping her foot. Adeline rubbed her crusty eyes and ran her fingers through the knots in her hair. Vivian squealed, startling Adeline. Suddenly, Adeline realized why. It was Vivian's birthday. For just a moment Adeline felt jealous that she didn't have a birthday of her own. However, she kept it to herself. This envious mood quickly vanished when Vivian gave Adeline a quick hug before hurrying off. The energy in Vivian's hug reminded Adeline of Jane.

Adeline got ready and put her mirror into her pocket. She strolled down the stairs trying to remember the dream that she had last night. Within minutes, Adeline toppled into Vivian who was waiting at the bottom of the stairs. Adeline apologized but Vivian pulled her to the kitchen. Adeline had taken longer than usual to get ready. She was trying to come up with a respectable story when the bell for Miss Low's room rang. Miss Nash rushed Vivian back upstairs and shoved Adeline towards the table, where she almost fell on Byron.

Adeline had occasionally run into a wall, but she had never been so klutzy in so little time. On top of that - it was only morning! Adeline raced upstairs to do her chores with a piece of cheese in hand. She had little time to eat. She desperately wanted this horrible day to end quickly.

* * *

Vivian missed supper. She was eating with Miss Low. Adeline thought it odd, but soon figured out why it wasn't. When Vivian arrived in the kitchen at the tail end of the meal, she was beaming her pearl smile.

Vivian entered the room wearing a tan jacket. The jacket had pins and what appeared to be badges down the arms. Vivian had acquired what looked to be a sewing badge, a service pin, and a few other things. Byron pretended not to be impressed and spoke of some of his achievements in a club he called "Boy Scouts." After hearing the exchange of adventures between the two, Adeline wanted in. She needed to be part of this thing called "Girl Scouts," but how?

It surprised Adeline that Miss Low allowed a servant into the group. Maybe Miss Low was different than the rest of the high society women and didn't think that they were beneath her? Vivian showed Miss Smith some of her badges. Miss Nash gave Vivian a basket which contained a needle, thread, cloth, a thimble, and some pins. Vivian thanked her and ran the present up to her room. It turned out that it wasn't such a bad day.

The next morning Adeline was awakened by the chirping of the birds outside her window instead of Vivian. As Adeline arrived in the kitchen she overheard Miss Nash talking to Miss Smith. They weren't whispering their conversation, but they weren't yelling it from the rooftops either.

"Vivian will be missing breakfast because she is setting up the living room for a Girl Scout meeting," Miss Nash said. "She's meeting her troop today."

"I heard that it is a small troop of only five girls," Miss Smith replied.

"Yes, now what is today's menu?" Miss Nash bellowed, clearly not trying to hide the conversation anymore.

It was time to eat and stop milling around. Adeline sat and tuned their conversations out of her head. She picked up her spoon and ate what seemed to be an attempt at oatmeal. It needed more liquid and was the exact opposite of the watery chili.

Adeline glanced at Byron and he was just sitting there playing with his food. He had bags under his eyes and looked tired. Adeline ate half of her breakfast and then found herself polishing silverware upstairs. Byron walked into the room and started helping her. He didn't say a word. Minutes passed. Adeline wanted to ask questions and make conversation, but she couldn't seem to break the silence. The bags under Byron's eyes seemed to be growing darker by the second. What happened last night, Adeline thought. Had he worked late? Or had he snuck out? A girl walked into the room and broke the silence.

The unknown girl came in giggling but stopped when she realized she had an audience. She looked to be the age of fourteen or fifteen and had a big bow nested in her brown hair. Usually you can tell when a person is sweet or sour, but with this girl one couldn't decide. She walked to the table to grab her book while smiling but swiftly exited with a questioning frown plastered onto her face. The smile tried to take over Adeline's face, but before it could Byron spoke.

Adeline asked Byron a question without saying a word. His eyes were clouded and he explained slowly, "I was up late last night looking out the window."

Adeline was about to change the topic when she realized that just looking out the window was not an everyday normal thing that a person would do. Adeline wondered what he meant by his words. Vague.

"I like to watch the movement of the carriages and people below," Byron murmured. "Then they decrease into the night. It's like my reflection time," Byron quieted his words this time as if embarrassed.

Adeline spoke more hushed too, "When I was an orphan. I would sing to some of my friends at night. I am a good singer, but then again, I have never heard anyone sing except for myself."

Byron smiled at this, loving that they had some secret of their own. This was not the first conversation that Adeline had expected to have had with Byron for he talked about his old life working as a page boy. He had worked at the household down the block. Adeline also told of her old life, seeing that it was her turn. The two of them bragged, complained, laughed, and quickly became good friends. By the time dinner came they had only completed half of their chores. They walked into the kitchen side by side, but quickly stopped.

The room was somber and sad. Vivian sat lonely at a table, while Rosemary and Miss Smith quietly cooked. Miss Nash was away dealing with some sort of meeting. Adeline sat down next to Vivian and asked her what was troubling her. Vivian was a Girl Scout, what more could she ask for. Right? Had something gone wrong in the meeting? Had Miss Low reconsidered allowing all girls into the group?

Byron went over to help Miss Smith with the cooking and Vivian sat silently staring straight ahead. Vivian's hands were folded neatly in her lap and her head was tilted slightly towards Adeline. She reminded Adeline of a sculpture, still and lifeless, just staring back at you with unblinking eyes.

Vivian responded after several minutes. Her voice was broken and dry, "My father is dead!"

Adeline recoiled pulling her hands from the table. She sought to comfort Vivian. Even though Vivian had known what it felt like to have a parent, now she was feeling the loss of losing one. Apparently, that was part of the package. Adeline felt like she got ripped off in her deal with partnership. She had gotten all of the loss and none of the love.

Byron stopped helping the others and sat down across from Vivian. This was all happening so fast. Vivian's eyes were glassy, and her sockets were puffy. She had been crying and might cry some more now. Vivian looked at the floor and silently wept. Adeline embraced her in an everlasting bearhug.

Byron sat still for he didn't know loss as well as Adeline did. He had only met loss once and it was over misplacing a silly rock. The rock was smooth and multicolored. The rock had a sibling, which Byron still had. He found the rocks with his older brother. Byron occasionally felt the rock, which was in his pocket. The rocks were not vital to his life or meaningful. He just loved the one that he still had, it was all that he had left from home. Now, Vivian had lost her family and Adeline had never even known her family. Byron felt guilty for being lucky and not noticing his blessings. He felt guilty for expecting and not appreciating, for talking and not listening.

Vivian cried on Adeline and tried to drain out the pain, but the discomfort stayed and became worse every second. Vivian's heart ached for her father's hugs. She yearned for a goodbye or warning. Right now, all Adeline wanted was for Vivian to feel better, but Adeline knew too well that pain would never leave. It will haunt you and taunt you. Pain will only leave when love returns.

Grass Stains and Spoons

A week had passed since Vivian's father died. Vivian was being eaten internally by pain. Adeline needed to get her friend's mind off of the pain because it was too…well, painful.

Adeline had today off and was planning on having some fun. Byron and Adeline planned to go outside and play sports and such. They invited Vivian, but she wanted to stay in her room. Adeline felt a gust of wind as she and Byron exited the kitchen. They had brought their breakfast and lunch in a basket, which Adeline held. Byron raced off towards the park, and Adeline followed not far behind. When they arrived, Adeline found a grassy spot by a tree covered in shade. They quickly ate their cold oatmeal breakfast. Adeline's hand dug into the damp grass and played with the soil underneath.

Byron walked over and approached some boys who were playing baseball. A fat boy with dirty blonde hair made bases out of rocks. He was carefully placing them as if the bases were masterpieces of art. They started playing with Byron as batter and the fat boy as pitcher.

Adeline hid the picnic basket underneath a bush and wondered why she couldn't play as well. After thinking some more about it, she stood. She walked down the hill. The hill was covered with random dirt patches and sticks. She almost tripped on a tree root, but finally reached the boys.

The oldest boy was tall and muscular, he was the leader. He noticed Adeline first and called a timeout. "What do you want?" the boy asked in a high-pitched voice, that didn't suit him. Adeline hesitated, but still asked to play.

All of the boys laughed and Byron adjusted his stance. He was becoming angry. Adeline stood closer to Byron, trying to make sure that he wouldn't pick a fight. It wasn't needed. She stood her ground and walked over to the bat that had been dropped on the field. Byron's anger turned into surprise, seeing that Adeline had the guts to live up to her word.

The wooden bat felt nice in her hands and she banged it onto the ground to get their attention. Some boys took their places, others left, and the leader took pitcher. He threw a fastball and she fouled. Again, he threw the baseball, but this time Adeline hit and ran to second base. Adeline enjoyed the adrenaline rush paired with the rocky grass floor of the park underneath her feet. Byron hit a home run and everyone cheered.

They told the boys that they had to leave after that. They wanted to do more with their day.

* * *

Byron and Adeline both had grass stains on their clothes when they left the game. Adeline only stained her apron and was thankful that her dress was saved. But she knew that they would get in trouble when they returned home. They walked, basket in hand, to a hidden pond a few blocks from the park. The water was clear. The sun was out, but they were protected by large swaying green trees. They again placed the basket under a bush and glanced to the sky to determine the time. They had to be home before dark and they still had a few hours left.

Byron took off his shoes and let his feet dangle in the cool water of the pond. Adeline did the same, carefully placing her socks inside her shoes. She had cut her stockings near the ankles and taken them off as if they were socks. "Could you sing something?" Byron asked.

"Yes, but how do you know that I can sing?" Adeline replied with suspicion.

"You look like someone who would be in a choir. Plus, you told me, silly goose," he reasoned.

Adeline smiled not knowing if that was a compliment or not. She started singing a song that reminded her of Vivian. It both saddened her and made her happy at the same time. The song held memories and could cast a spell on you.

After the song finished they sat for a minute, silent, watching the ripples in the crystal, clear pond. Byron suddenly jumped up and ran to the picnic basket. He hung it on a tree branch and started climbing a tree. He stopped when he found a good place to sit. Adeline raced after him thinking that something bad would jump out at her if she stayed on the ground.

"Today we will enjoy the view and have some tea," Byron shouted, proud of himself. He handed her a metal bottle that was filled to the top with once warm tea.

The perch they sat on looked out onto the pond. They sat on a wide branch, with leaves overhead. Though they had a clear view, Adeline slowly settled in with her back against the trunk of the tree. It was relaxing here. It was still daylight, but she eventually fell asleep.

* * *

Adeline awoke with Byron slumped next to her and the sun hanging low in the sky. It's a wonder they didn't fall from the large branch they were balanced upon. Her hand was laid out on the coarse bark with Byron's fingertips ever so slightly touching the tips of her fingers. She shook Byron awake and together they carefully climbed down from the tree and raced home.

When they arrived back at the house the sun was setting, and they were both panting and sweating. Adeline felt a pain in her upper arm and saw that she had a bleeding cut. Byron tied a piece of fabric around the cut as they walked in the door. Miss Smith was cooking, and Miss Nash was waiting at attention ready to loom over them.

Miss Nash meticulously looked them up and down and started complaining, "You two are out gallivanting while we continue to work hard! Look at the grass stains on your clothes. They were new! So ungrateful."

Miss Nash took a wooden spoon out of Miss Smith's hand. Miss Smith had been using it to stir boiling hot soup, so the spoon was still hot to the touch. Miss Nash's complaints turned fiercer now that she had a weapon to wield at them. The words flew from her mouth like venom from a snake.

Miss Nash chose her words carefully. Her goal was not to hurt them, but merely prick or sting them. While Miss Nash was talking Adeline saw Vivian looming in the doorway. She was about to signal to Vivian to leave, when Adeline felt a hot wooden spoon slap her hand. It left a large red mark. Byron tried to say something but before he could he received a mark that matched Adeline's. Adeline's upper arm and hand were stinging. It was weakening her. The pain seemed to travel up her arm. She didn't have the strength to protect Byron or herself. She just took the marks on her hands as battle scars.

Adeline caught a glance of the cut on her arm, which was still bleeding. It looked like someone had taken a chunk out of her arm. It was two or three inches long and was covered in a combination of splinters, dirt, sweat, and her own blood. The cut was visible through a hole in Adeline's dress. The fabric that Byron had tied around was turning scarlet and the opposite of its once white state. Miss Nash adjusted her stance and Adeline could see Vivian preparing a new bandage in the doorway already.

Byron looked down at his feet. His shoes were thrown on sloppily. They had to be slipped on in their rush home. Adeline flinched as she received another mark from Miss Nash for not listening. After some more minutes Miss Nash finally stopped. She set the deadly spoon down and exited suddenly.

* * *

Vivian rung out a cloth she had drenched in a healing solution and set it on Adeline's wound. Byron had put aloe on their marks to help dial down the pain. It was a new day. This meant that Vivian had to change Adeline's bandage, and Adeline needed to complete her chores. Their two-day break was over. They spent the day consoling Vivian and explaining what had happened on Byron and Adeline's adventure. The only thing that they left out was all the tree climbing business. Adeline's wound wasn't healing too well. Vivian's Girl Scout remedies were helping, but they weren't enough. Then again it had only been a day or two and they all knew that the wound wouldn't heal instantly.

Today they had tea and leftovers for breakfast. To get into specifics Byron had chicken soup and stale bread. Vivian had cold chili and crackers. Adeline had bacon fat with a buttered biscuit. The buttered biscuit was somewhat fresh and tasted wonderful, but the bacon fat was greasy and chewy. Life was finally going steady for once. Adeline felt like she could sit back and relax. Even though it would be improper to do so, things just seemed to be right somehow.

5

Dreams and Realities

On this morning Adeline was awoken by Byron instead of Vivian. Adeline pulled the covers over her head and nuzzled into her warm bed. She had just dreamt the loveliest dream. She had been flying above the world. She had seen her neighborhood from the sky. It was as if she were a bird, swooshing through the air, but without the help of a flying machine. Byron cleared his throat and Adeline uncurled from the scratchy wool blanket that she had been using.

Byron walked down to the kitchen and Adeline got ready. She held onto her mirror tightly. It felt like she hadn't touched the precious object in forever. If Adeline didn't have her mirror, then she would be lost. She turned it over in her hands slowly. A very aged "AW" was engraved faintly on the handle. Strange. She had never noticed that before. Adeline pushed the thought away. Her hair was horribly knotty. She had to get dressed quickly so she had enough time to brush through the rat's nest on her head called hair.

By the time Adeline was done there were clumps of her hair covering the floor. She raced to the kitchen and grabbed an apple. She would have to eat and work because of the extra time that she had taken getting ready. As Adeline cleaned a worn wooden cabinet with a feather duster she saw a streak of blonde rush by in the hallway. Byron had either been spying on her or quickly passing by. Adeline knew that it was probably the latter, but secretly wished that it was closer to the former. She shook her head at herself and sneezed as dust flew in her face.

Adeline quickly put the dirtied duster down as Byron entered the room. He was dressed up in a nice jacket and for once was wearing untorn pants. This was fancy for him, but casual for most folks. He held a grin on his face and a newsboy cap in his hand. Adeline casually rested a hand on her hip, unimpressed.

Byron saw a question in her eyes and answered. "This won't get us into any more trouble. Don't worry." His voice sounded excited and Adeline still wondered why.

"Why are you grinning like a fool?" she joked.

Byron grinned and then disappeared in a swift run. Adeline frowned, puzzled. Then she woke up. She must have dusted herself to sleep. She was curled up by the fireplace.

Adeline stood and brushed some stray ashes from her dress. She stashed her forgotten duster into her pocket and went to look at the window. She had slept for far too long, dinner would be soon. What was with her lately?

Adeline walked down the hallway, her shoes silently slapping the wooden floor. She saw Vivian passing by and smiled. Adeline had not seen Vivian much since her father's death, but she wasn't heartless and gave Vivian her time with a reassuring smile.

It must be so hard for Vivian, she thought. Vivian smiled back unexpectedly and waved. Adeline and Vivian scurried down to the kitchen together, laughing on the way.

* * *

After a dinner of watery chili, Adeline walked lazily to her room. Vivian waved goodnight just as Adeline closed her bedroom door. Soon, Adeline heard a whisper and turned to look at the door but saw nothing in the room with her. Before she could figure out what was going on Adeline's door briskly opened, and she let out a surprised scream. Byron entered, and she relaxed. He apologized for disturbing her while Adeline composed herself again.

Tomorrow is Adeline's birthday and somehow Byron already knows.

"So, tomorrow is your birthday. We don't get a break so that makes playing baseball impossible," Byron says with a hand on his temple.

"We could share our chores to get the work done quicker. Then we would have extra time," Adeline suggests.

Byron leans against Adeline's now closed door. He tries to think of ideas but doesn't share any of them.

Most of the ideas Adeline will not tolerate since she doesn't enjoy breaking the rules and neither does Byron. Byron slumps his shoulders with his back still against the door and Adeline sits down on her bed resting her chin in her hands.

Minutes of silence passed before Adeline's Bible fell off her shelf and hit the floor loudly. Byron put it back on the shelf and sat down next to Adeline. He was about to speak when Adeline's door creaked open and revealed a flustered Rosemary. She nearly dropped her candle when her eyes rested on Byron. Byron rushed to the door and carefully pulled her into the room. He then closed the door again behind her.

Rosemary was still in shock. "Sorry if I was interrupting something. I just heard a noise and…" she trailed off. Rosemary tried to retreat back towards the door, but Byron blocked her escape path.

"It is not what it looks like. We were just planning for my birthday tomorrow," Adeline explained.

Rosemary blinked like she was expecting something more. "Okay well then.. I will just go back to bed," Rosemary shyly said after she realized that Adeline was done explaining.

Byron moved away from the door while saying, "Oh, and please don't tell anyone of this visit. Thanks! Goodnight."

Rosemary slipped away through the door, her long hair waving like a flag behind her. Byron sighed and locked the door.

Adeline was exhausted. "All of this work for a simple birthday," she said sighing and laying her head on the wall behind her bed. Byron sat down next to her again. She silently screamed when their shoulders brushed. They sat some more in silence. It was a nice silence.

"I better go, I don't want to fall asleep and have Vivian find me here in the morning."

"Yeah," Adeline simply replied.

Byron stood and awkwardly walked to the door. Adeline resisted a smile.

"Oh, and how do you know about my birthday?" Adeline asked sitting up.

"I knew a boy from the orphanage next door to yours. He knew everything about all of you girls. It was a little creepy if you ask me," Byron said stopping mid stride.

"Who," she asked.

Byron hesitated and said, "I'll explain more tomorrow. Okay?" And with that he disappeared into the hallway.

* * *

Morning came too soon. Adeline felt so tired. She felt a sharp pain in her arm and took off the bandage covering her wound. It was turning an eerie, yellow color and was surely infected. She got another bandage that Vivian gave to her. Adeline put it on herself using some ointment and tape. She ran down to the kitchen. No one had awoken her today and it was her birthday. Come on really?

It wasn't very early but there was no one in the kitchen. The floor creaked under Adeline's feet and her stomach churned. She helped herself to some cold oatmeal left on the table and a glass of water. After she finished eating she washed the dishes. An old scrap of paper caught her eye and Adeline saw that someone had left a note on the table.

It read:

HAPPY BIRTHDAY ADELINE -B

She immediately knew the message was from Byron. This must be his plan for her birthday. After taking a moment to try to figure things out, Adeline spotted Vivian's head visible from behind a table off in the distance. Adeline pretended that she didn't notice Vivian. They must all be in on it. Interesting. Next, the door swung open and Adeline's heart started racing. This was supposed to be a birthday present so why should it scare her?

A basket was sitting on the steps through the open door. It was tied shut with a silver ribbon. The contents of the basket were covered with a jade colored cloth. The color faintly reminded Adeline of her mirror. She welcomed the mysterious gift and sat down on the cold steps to open it. Inside the present were six tiny boxes. Adeline untied the ribbon on the first box. After some struggle she was finally able to open the box.

It was from Vivian. The box contained a small bottle of perfume about the length of Adeline's pinky and the width of her thumb. It smelled sweet and was a pretty blue color.

The second box was from Miss Smith. Inside the box was a small skeleton key. Adeline knew it would open every room in the house, so she had to be careful who she showed this to. She put her finds in the basket and reached for the third box.

The next box was from Miss Nash. The box was darker than the others, more worn and loved. Inside was a bundle of photos. The photos showed a young Miss Low, Miss Nash, and Miss Smith. They all looked pretty in matching church dresses. Miss Nash was the youngest, while Miss Low appeared to be the oldest by a year or two. It was amazing how much you could tell about a person from their photographs.

The fourth box was from Rosemary. The box was enveloped in a red ribbon. Adeline could use that in her hair. Inside of the box were more ribbons and hair pins. They were all the colors of the rainbow and smelled of kitchen spices.

A fifth box was from Byron. The box itself looked ordinary. Inside the box was a journal. It was kelly green with gold trim. A note was inscribed on the inside.

It read:

HAPPY BIRTHDAY!

USE THIS JOURNAL TO WRITE DOWN ALL OF YOUR EXPERIENCES. DON'T FORGET TO INCLUDE OUR PICNIC!

Adeline turned the book over in her hands and then set it down with the rest of her gifts. That was so nice of Byron. How did he save up enough money to buy such a fancy book? She would start writing in it as soon as she could.

The sixth and final box was larger than the others. The box alone was a gift in and of itself. There was a metal clasp holding the box closed that required a key to open it. Adeline took out the skeleton key and opened the box. It was a perfect fit.

Inside, the box was lined with soft cushions. There was a letter inside of the box as well. It was from Miss Low and was written in fancy cursive handwriting. Adeline pulled the letter out of the envelope and read it in her head.

Dear Adeline,

I hear that you are a very good worker and have the best of spirits. Happy Birthday!

Sincerely,
Miss Low

Adeline planned on putting her mirror in the special box that Miss Low gave her. She felt that it was an honor to receive the letter and wondered if Vivian had received a similar gift for her birthday.

A pan clattered to the floor behind Adeline and she rushed to pick up her basket. She slowly sat down at the table and tried to spot the other's hiding spots. She had no luck.

Soon enough, Vivian casually walked out from her hiding place and wished Adeline a happy birthday. Then she grabbed a bowl of oatmeal for breakfast. Rosemary was next, followed by Miss Smith. Then Byron and finally Miss Nash. It was hard to imagine

Miss Nash hiding in the shadows behind an antique piece of furniture, yet Adeline succeeded.

Adeline put her basket under the chair to make way for breakfast after she thanked everyone. Byron tapped her on the shoulder and asked her if she liked her gifts. Adeline smiled and hugged him. She didn't know if a hug was too little or too much. Vivian came over and joined them in hugging. Before they knew it everyone in the kitchen was in a giant group hug. Miss Nash somehow still managed to look ladylike and elegant even with Miss Smith's arms thrown about her.

Adeline for once felt loved and special. She had never loved being herself as much as she did at this very moment. She feared that if she blinked this fantasy of a life would vanish before her eyes.

Lots of scents hit Adeline while she was being hugged. She smelled Miss Smith's soups and Miss Nash's perfume, Vivian's mint scented hair, and Byron's smile. Adeline didn't know how to smell a smile, but somehow she did. Adeline was mad at herself. She had felt like she was someone with a sad past, a past to weep about. Now she realized how lucky she really was. Adeline could take in the feelings, emotions, and smells.

"This is where I belong…" Adeline thought to herself, "…in this small kitchen surrounded with people I love."

She felt Byron's heart beat against hers. She felt Vivian's hair rest on her shoulder. She felt Miss Smith's arms wrapping around them all, uniting them. She was lucky. She is lucky. Hopefully, she'll stay lucky.

6

Feelings and Fights

Vivian scurried into the living room and snuck up behind Adeline. Adeline was so concentrated on sewing a ripped pillow that she didn't even notice Vivian. Adeline loved the way the silver thread sparkled while the needle glided neatly through the pillow. She finally noticed Vivian and invited her to sit down and help. Vivian looked more excited than anyone in history had ever looked over the task of mending a pillow.

"I have news," Vivian said with a giddy voice, "and I can't figure out if it is good or bad yet?"

Adeline put her work aside and rested her chin in her hand. "Proceed," Adeline urged.

So many thoughts raced through Adeline's head, but none of them quite fit into the puzzle.

"So, yesterday before your birthday party we hid. Remember?"

Adeline nodded her head in recognition of Vivian.

"I was about to hide when Byron came up to me. He was acting weird that day. He was talking to me differently. More polite and formal. So, I didn't think anything of it. I had assumed that he had just been anxious because of your party."

Adeline bobbed her head as Vivian spilled, "Alright, well then after the party he was acting all joking like. You could have even mistaken it for flirting."

"Vivian, really? Just because of some strange conversations now you think Byron fancies you?" Adeline said while rolling her eyes.

Leave it to Vivian to make up a romance. Why did it bother Adeline so much? It was just some stupid suggestion.

"Yeah and I mean it wouldn't be half bad if he did. He is kind of cute," Vivian said trying to back herself up.

Adeline directed her rage towards the sofa and gripped the seat cushion. Vivian was caught up in her own thoughts about Byron and didn't seem to notice. Vivian continued and made a big speech, while Adeline sat watching it all go down.

This was all so confusing. Did Adeline like Byron? Did Byron like Vivian? Did Vivian like Byron? Byron and Vivian were both perfect. They could practically be the dream couple when they got older. Adeline hoped that they didn't get together. Yes, she wanted them both to be happy, but hopefully fate could be rewritten.

* * *

Adeline walked down the hall. Her shoes clapped the unpolished servant's floors. She was going to see Byron. Adeline needed to sort things out, even if it meant telling Byron that Vivian liked him. As she approached she saw a figure with blood red hair standing in the doorway. It was Vivian who paced back and forth outside of Byron's door.

"You can't come in yet," Vivian quickly shouted while waving her hands in the air.

"Oh, so now you're his bodyguard?" Adeline spoke without thinking. She tried to conceal the anger in her tone. She immediately took it all back. She just wanted to see Byron, not start a fight with Vivian.

"Why do you care?" Vivian spat her words.

Adeline had to backpedal fast, even though she wanted to stick up for herself.

"I'm sorry Vivian. I'm just anxious," Adeline said falsely.

"Why?" Vivian half yelled. Her anger wasn't faltering.

"To…um…discuss important matters," Adeline spoke with hesitation in her voice. Vivian looked flustered.

"Well then, you will have to wait like me," Adeline was confused that Vivian had to wait. She had just assumed that she was debating on whether to enter or not.

"Okay, but why?" Adeline asked.

"I don't know, he just said to wait! Now get in line!"

"Wow!" Adeline exclaimed loudly as she was taken back by Vivian's words and unkind tone.

This was getting a lot more complicated than she had wanted it to be. Why was Vivian waiting? Was

Byron playing a joke on her? And since when did they both answer to Byron?

Maybe Byron was stalling Vivian and seeing if she would just go away. If so, why would he do that? Just as another question popped into Adeline's head the door eased open and Byron emerged.

Adeline didn't know why Vivian was mad at her. Adeline hadn't discouraged Vivian's feelings for Byron, or at least not yet because that would be too cruel. Adeline could not decide her own opinion of the matter.

Byron was still in his work clothes, but his nightclothes were ready and spread on his bed. Byron was tired and simply wanted rest after this long day of work. Vivian had been bugging him. She had been acting like an annoying sister. He already had many young cousins to take care of at home, he didn't need another one. As Vivian looked at Byron she expected him to thank her for waiting, or for him to prompt her on. He didn't. He just stood there looking between the two of them.

When no one spoke, Byron injected his thoughts, "Well, if you two have nothing to say to me, then I am going to bed."

Vivian frowned and just stood there. As Byron was about to close the door Adeline stopped him. She jammed her foot in between the door and wall, forcing him to keep it open.

"Wait!" she yelled.

Byron turned and reopened the door again, sighing. Vivian scowled at Adeline. Adeline could grab Byron's attention easily.

"It seems like Adeline can control Byron," Vivian thought bitterly to herself. Her scowl deepened.

Adeline was a year younger than both Byron and Vivian. Would that make her seem less mature? That would be bad, right?

"We all have something to discuss!" Adeline blurted out, sounding very official.

Byron motioned for them to come in with his hand. He seemed to understand what Adeline had meant even though he never possibly could. Could he? Did he know why they were here? He had probably overheard them in the hall. This whole situation suddenly felt off, but it was real life.

Byron closed the door behind them and Vivian let out a small squeak. Adeline ignored it and so did Byron. It was almost curfew. They had to hurry this talk up. Byron shoved his night clothes off the bed, wrinkling his sheets in the process. Adeline leaned on the door. She didn't want Rosemary walking in again. Vivian sat down on another bed opposite from Byron. Byron's room had two twin beds. Byron sighed again and leaned his back against the peeling white walls. Vivian faced Byron and took a breath.

Vivian begun, "So, Adeline fancies you and she is jealous that she doesn't get all of your attention."

Adeline shot Vivian a dirty look. "I didn't say that," Adeline said calmly.

Vivian whined, "Well, then, what does he think?"

Byron looked between the two of them dumbfound. "I have never been asked permission for someone to like me before," Byron responded

Why did Vivian even have to bring this up to

Byron? Adeline focused on her thoughts instead of Vivian's scowling face.

"Why did we have to talk to Byron about this?" Adeline inquired. It felt good to voice her thoughts.

"He has every right to hear all of this conversation. Even if he may not be needed!"

Vivian was getting so annoying. "He has a name!" Adeline yelled finally, breaking her cool. Vivian was lying and even she knew it.

Byron sat up and walked over to Adeline. He sat down at her side.

"You have to calm down or you will wake up the whole house," he whispered.

Adeline relaxed with Byron at her side. She liked being in his presence; it soothed her nerves. Vivian eyed them with envy. Byron noticed and scooted away from Adeline a bit. The crushing weight of reality sunk in again. Adeline's nerves blossomed.

Vivian got up and stormed across the room. When Vivian had finished pouting she sat down next to Byron, on his other side. Byron inched closer to Adeline once more, before getting up and walking over to where Vivian had been seated before.

Vivian blew up. This was like musical chairs. She started yelling. She didn't care if she woke up the entire house.

Vivian lashed out at Adeline, "You think that you are perfect. You think that you are everything that Byron would ever want, Adeline. You are just immature. Lucky for you Byron is too. Sooner, or later, he will grow up and be able to see clearly. He will see that you are just a child caught up in your own daydreams."

With that Vivian paraded out of the room. Adeline stood. She was still absorbing all the words that Vivian had said. Vivian had meant those words. Vivian was right. Adeline was and will forever be a dreamer. Was that a bad thing?

Did that mean that no one would ever like her? If no one would like her, then how could someone love her? Adeline felt no tears in her eyes. She felt no urge to cry. All she felt was anger. All she felt was hate. All she felt was Vivian. All she felt was her ignorance. All she felt was her childness. All she felt was regret. All she felt was the truth.

Adeline left the room. She didn't care that Byron was calling her name. She slammed her bedroom door in his face and threw the contents of her shelf onto the floor. Adeline felt a pain in her arm and saw that her bandage was soaked through with greenish, yellowish pus. Suddenly a wave of dizziness washed over her.

The world went spinning in slow motion. She stumbled to her bed. She needed to ground herself. Byron knocked on the door and eventually got in. By then Adeline was almost to her bed. It was so far away. She leaned this way and that way. Suddenly Adeline fell into Byron's arms. Everything went black. Reality is crushing. Reality is the truth. Reality is darkness.

7

Loss and a Fever

Adeline awoke on Venus. The sun burned her eyes. She was caked in dried sweat from the heat. Something cool touched her forehead and her eyes focused. Miss Smith stood before Adeline, holding a damp cloth to Adeline's head.

Adeline was in her room and Byron stood at the doorway. Miss Nash had been there too but left as soon as Adeline showed signs of life. Vivian stuck her head through the door but also left when Byron gave her a look.

Adeline was changed into a cotton nightgown. It was white with gold trimming. Adeline thought she must be dying. They would never give her anything this nice to wear in bed otherwise.

"Miss Low sent it when she heard what happened," Miss Smith explained.

"It would have been nice of her to send a doctor too, but we can only hope for so much." Adeline couldn't believe the ungratefulness came from her own mouth. She must not be feeling well at all.

Adeline tried to sit up and winced. Her arm was now unbandaged and just as she began to feel some relief, Adeline bent her arm and cracked the still fresh scab. The pus oozed out like a waterfall. Her blanket had a yellow stain from where her arm had been lying and it smelled horrible. The contents of her shelves were no longer on the floor. They were put back neatly as if they had never been touched.

Miss Smith got Adeline a fresh glass of water, then left. Byron was left standing in the doorway. Adeline's body ached with exhaustion. He turned around as if to walk away, but Adeline shouted, "Get back here!"

Before leaving the room, Byron made an about face turn and replied in a dry voice, "You look like you have lived in the wild for all of your life!"

Byron sat down at the foot of Adeline's bed as she rolled her eyes.

"Thanks. That is just what I wanted to hear," Adeline replied, sarcastically. "But what really happened?" she asked.

"Well, you sort of just fell into my arms like the girls do in the movies."

Adeline laughed at this. "In your dreams!" she replied to his nonsense.

Byron crossed his legs and smiled. "No, seriously you were awake one second and then asleep the next." Byron made a motion with his hands of her walking around and then falling over.

"And?" Adeline laughed. She was almost enjoying his explanation of her downfall.

"Then I brought you to Miss Smith and now you are here," Byron explained.

Miss Nash burst through the door and Byron abruptly stood up. "And what do you think you are doing in the girls' quarters, let alone a sick girl's quarters?" Miss Nash boomed, while pointing an accusing finger at Byron.

"Nothing ma'am," Byron said. Now, he was all business.

"Good, because you were just leaving," Miss Nash grabbed Byron by the ear and marched him out of the room. It was suddenly lonely again.

Adeline could hear droplets of rain beating softly on the roof. Quickly she became very cold, but the cold didn't last long. Heat flooded in and Adeline broke into a sweat. How had she been sleeping only a few minutes ago? Now it seemed impossible to rest. Adeline tried to focus on the patter of rain outside that was slowly growing louder. It seemed to drown out her senses and she slowly drifted to sleep.

* * *

The next morning a face loomed above her and something tickled her cheek. Apparently waking up to an audience was Adeline's new hobby. Vivian looked down at Adeline, her hair had come undone and now grazed Adeline's face. Vivian mumbled something before scurrying away. It sounded like,

"I'm Sammy?" No, that wasn't right. "I'm sorry?" Yes, maybe that was it. Why would Vivian say sorry? It was clear now that Vivian disliked Adeline.

Did Byron say something to her about it? No, he wouldn't have. Would he? Adeline's head spun with questions so much that it was giving her a headache. Miss Smith brought her a tray of food and then hurried back to work. The tray was polished and worth more than Adeline could ever hope to earn in her lifetime. She ate in silence. The only sound was Adeline chewing on her stale bread and slowly eating her soup. It was hard to eat. Taking in this nourishment seemed to upset her stomach. It was already doing somersaults on its own.

Adeline set the half-eaten bowl of soup back on the tray. She pushed the tray to the foot of her bed and found her brush and mirror lying nearby. Her hair was a mess. Adeline killed some time by getting the knots out of her hair. By the end of it she had somewhat presentable hair again. She had shed in the process and was surrounded by lumps of her knots.

* * *

Several days had passed and Adeline had slowly recovered from her sickness. The cut on her arm was just a mere pinkish scab. It was around dinner time and Adeline limped down to the kitchen on aching legs. She was the first to get to the table. For completing this task she was awarded with warm soup - not hot soup, but warm soup. It was good enough.

Byron was seated next. Vivian came sulking in last.

Adeline had healed, but Vivian was still wounded. Vivian's eyes looked like they were made of crystals. She had been crying and a thin layer of tears still stained her face. However, Vivian's clothes were unwrinkled and spotless. It was as if she had been doing laundry in her spare time. Adeline finished the last of her soup and accepted another half-filled bowl of broth. Byron was eating slowly and playing with his food. It looked like he could feel Vivian's struggle as if it was his own. The adults were oblivious and just assumed that everyone was tired. It was going to be a long week.

Learning and Listening

Adeline tucked her pillow under the wool blanket and made her bed. She could not believe that Miss Low, the Juliette Gordon Low, had requested an audience with her today. She wanted to make sure that everything looked sharp. Adeline pinned her hair up into a neat bun. It had grown long since the time when she first arrived. Adeline hid a piece of lavender in her pocket. She had taken it from the kitchen in an attempt to make herself smell fresher.

Adeline's candle was still lit in its porcelain white holder. As she quickly snuffed the flames out it left a faint trail of smoke. There was no time for breakfast today as Adeline hurried quickly down the stairs. She approached a large wooden door that looked intimidating at first glance. The door opened swiftly because it was well oiled.

Miss Low's office was big. A large wooden desk sat in the middle of the room housing a manly looking armchair. Lace curtains lined the three windows and bookcases covered the walls. Photos and paintings hung all around the room with golden frames. Miss Low wore a long-sleeved, plaid dress with a matching overcoat. Black lace accents frilled on her torso and were peeking out from under her jacket. Brown lace-up boots fashioned her feet while white socks laid underneath them.

Adeline stood before Miss Low, awed and nervous. She had to clamp down her hands behind her back in order to keep them from shaking. Miss Low stepped out from behind her desk and leaned on the old wooden surface of its face. The color gray overtook Miss Low's once brown hair. It was tied back into a military style bun.

"Sit, dear!" Miss Low beckoned.

Adeline did as she was told and sat down in a oversized velvet chair. The chair itself must have been expensive, not to mention the entire room. How could she afford it all?

Miss Low sat down and put on a pair of reading glasses. She picked up a piece of paper.

"Adeline," she read aloud. "She is a speedy worker and a bright girl. She almost always follows the rules, except when distracted by others."

It had been noted that she was especially distracted around Byron. The report had clearly been written by Miss Nash. Adeline's cheeks tinted pink. Miss Low smirked but continued to read the paper.

"She is close friends with Vivian or was. She is still just as qualified as Vivian to become a Girl Scout."

Miss Low paused and Adeline's heart beat in double time. She slid the paper away and placed her hands on top of her big desk.

All that Adeline could do was stare, trying to steady her breathing. A tense silence passed before Miss Low smiled. She stood suddenly and gave Adeline an embrace. Miss Low handed Adeline a uniform. "Now hurry girl, you have your first meeting in an hour's time. Put the uniform on and meet me in the living room," she said while pushing Adeline out the door.

Adeline's breath was still rapid. She was going to be a Girl Scout! Not just any Girl Scout, but one of the first ever!

* * *

Vivian's feet pounded down the hallway in a steady rhythm. She was already in her uniform and heading towards Adeline's room. She was supposed to be bringing Adeline to her first meeting. Oh, and of course Adeline *had* to be in Vivian's Troop.

The door swung open. Adeline stood wearing a tan overcoat and skirt, paired with dress shoes and knee high socks. Her jacket was unadorned. It held no badges or pins yet. She held a matching tan hat in her white gloved hands. The uniform felt stiff and new. She had to break it in and get used to the almost military like feeling. Vivian started to walk down the hall and Adeline followed. Neither of them talked to each other. The only sound was the echo of their footsteps in sync with one another.

When they arrived in the living room, three other girls were already gathered there. Miss Low gestured to an open seat and Adeline took it. Vivian sat across from her on a sofa with one of the other girls. Two of the girls sat next to Adeline as well. All of them displayed the many achievements they had earned on their jackets' sleeves, each merit represented by a special pin or badge. Each one of their jackets said something about that girl's interests and what was unique to her as a person. Maybe Adeline could earn badges of her own one day? How many would she be able to get?

"Now girls, this is Adeline. She is a new addition to our family," Miss Low said this with an unusually nurturing voice.

Adeline waved a hand. As if they needed to know who she was, she stuck out like a sore thumb.

"Hello, Adeline!" all the girls said in unison. Their hands were folded on their laps and their legs were angled slightly to the right. It was as if the girls were all one person, except spread amongst different bodies.

The girl to Adeline's right spoke quickly. "Hi, my name is Lauren." She was a small girl and looked younger than her age. She had light brown hair that looked like butterscotch. It was tied up in a loose ponytail. Glasses rested on the bridge of her nose and she fiddled with them every now and then. Her jacket had many cooking badges on it. She also had a bronze pin.

To Adeline's left sat a girl with pale skin and dark black hair that hung upon her shoulders. "I'm Mareena," she said in a firm and steady voice. She had a calm, almost zen-like presence to her.

Unlike Lauren, Mareena had mostly needlework

badges and other artsy things, such as what looked to be paint brushes or watercolors.

Adeline looked now to Vivian. Vivian's jacket was scattered with a variety of things from housework to horseback riding.

Next to Vivian was a tall girl. Her uniform was clearly used and had some sewn up patches here and there. "My name is Clover and I have been a Girl Scout longer than any of you."

Adeline observed her jacket. It was filled to the brim with badges. Vivian gave Adeline a bittersweet smile. The tension between them lingered. Clover seemed to be Vivian's new best friend and as much as that bothered Adeline she refused to show it. Adeline put a hand to her mouth to cover a fabricated yawn. She had already moved on.

Miss Low handed her a textbook. It was so heavy Adeline nearly dropped it. "This is a book full of the basics. You have already earned some merits, and get others when you join us," Miss Low explained.

Adeline had to study up and quickly.

"Now open up your books to chapter three girls. Today, we will be continuing our lesson on painting." Miss Low's voice captured Adeline's attention

Adeline opened the musty book to page 200 and reviewed the lesson summary.

It read:

This lesson will help a young woman become educated in the arts, specifically painting (such as oil paintings versus acrylic paintings) as well as some powerful women figures in painting.

Adeline sighed as Miss Low started to read the passage. After a wasted twenty minutes, they set the book aside and took out some paint brushes, along with the other necessary materials: paint, an easel, a canvas, and a reference.

The reference was a picture of a dark bedroom. In the bedroom there was a window that shed some light in from the outside and lessened the darkness. It reminded Adeline of her old life. It spoke of how quickly the light could take over the dark. Or how quickly the dark could take over the light. She started to paint and finally became engaged.

9

Vivian and a Visitor

It was a day after the meeting and Adeline was tired. Her hands were sore from painting and her brain yearned for a moment of rest. It was breakfast time and she had woken up early today to have time to eat. Adeline was sitting at the table with a bowl of oatmeal in hand. There was a knock at the back door and everyone tensed. Adeline tossed her oatmeal aside and readied herself to answer the door. It was in the far right corner of the kitchen, away from where Adeline was stationed. Vivian beat her to the door and opened it promptly.

"Mom!" she cried out as she hugged the figure in the doorway.

Adeline tried to mind her own business, but it wasn't a crime to eavesdrop once and awhile.

"Hi, Vivian!" her mother staggered through joyful tears. "Guess who I found?" she continued. Vivian gave her mother a confused look. A girl stepped out from behind Vivian's mother. Adeline was able to make out a blurred figure in the dim light.

"Hello," said a sweet familiar voice.

Adeline quickly wondered why the voice sounded so familiar. Suddenly, Adeline recognized who it was. Jane! It was Adeline's old best friend from the orphanage. Adeline stood from her chair, nearly spilling the now cold oatmeal. Vivian's mother continued to talk as Jane made eye contact with Adeline. They both stayed frozen in the shock of recognition.

"This is your long, lost sister. Her name is Jane. When she was born we hit a rough patch. We had no choice and gave her up for adoption. We told the orphanage that we would come back for her when she turned thirteen. By then we figured that we would have proper money.

"The orphanage didn't tell Jane any of this, so she had believed that I was dead. She didn't even know that today was her birthday! It really is an outrage. So, I came and picked her up today. Then, I signed her up for a job interview here, in hopes that she could work with her newly found sister."

Vivian let out an unladylike squeal when her mother finished. She hugged Jane and welcomed her with openness. Adeline walked over to them, abandoning her seat.

Jane looked different, older. Jane let go of Vivian and embraced Adeline. A foolish grin was plastered on Jane's face all the while. They all celebrated in a fit of smiles and hugs after Adeline explained how she knew Jane.

Jane and her mother stayed overnight in the extra quarters. Jane was to have a brief interview. She was to be trying out for the position of maid. If she was hired, then she would be able to stay with Adeline and Vivian. This meant that Jane would have to leave her mother, who she had just reunited with. Adeline digested all of this as she laid in bed.

* * *

It was early in the morning, about two. That was three hours earlier than Adeline usually would have woken up. It seemed that she was getting into a bad habit of night pondering. She pushed off her blanket and took her mirror off the shelf. It had grown dusty, so Adeline wiped it off gingerly with a cloth. Then she set it down on her bed. She washed her face with water from a basin. She used the still clean side of the cloth to wipe the droplets from her face.

Today was going to be a special day. Jane's interview was a full day of working in the house. Adeline would have to show Jane the inner workings of the home. That meant that Adeline would have to work hand in hand with Vivian.

Vivian and Adeline were still on shaky terms right now. How did Jane feel about all of this? She had just found her new family. What about her father's death? How did Vivian feel? Adeline didn't even know how she felt anymore. It had been a rollercoaster of emotions for everyone. It was like a ride that you wanted to get off but couldn't.

After Adeline finished her morning routine she walked down to the kitchen.

"An early riser today," commented Miss Smith, upon seeing Adeline.

Adeline shrugged feeling more like a confused owl. Miss Smith gave her a sympathetic look as if reading Adeline's mind.

"Cheer up, child. Tomorrow is going to be a good day. You just have to stick it out," Miss Smith reassured her as she handed Adeline a fresh bowl of oatmeal.

What will be happening tomorrow? Adeline had no more time to think. With that thought, Jane burst into the kitchen, full of energy. She seemed determined to get the job and Adeline respected her for that. Adeline patted a chair that Jane could sit in.

Jane beamed with excitement and Adeline attempted a smile. Adeline felt off today. She was on edge. It was odd seeing Jane here, after so many years of memories only in the orphanage together.

"Now we just have to wait for the others and then I can share the news," Miss Smith bellowed with a giddy voice.

What could Miss Smith be talking about? The others eventually filtered into the kitchen. When everyone arrived Miss Smith cleared her throat. Miss Nash was the only one who didn't look to be on edge. She probably already knew. Adeline sat on the edge of her seat, filled with curiosity.

"We will be preparing for a banquet tomorrow…" Miss Smith paused momentarily, "…a banquet which we all will be allowed to attend."

Several concerned looks were exchanged while Miss Nash finished.

"Miss Low wants to extend her invitation to even the lowliest people. She has kindly provided some new outfits for us as well."

After a few moments of hesitation, loud cheering began. This proposition was highly unorthodox, but it was really happening.

"Today we will have to set up the decor, cook the food, and go to the clothes' fitting," Miss Smith commanded.

Rosemary grabbed a list and started to prepare a dish. Byron jumped up as well. He carried a basket full of napkins, tablecloths, and lace upstairs. Jane looked to Vivian for something to do but got no response. Adeline stood and Jane followed.

Adeline lugged another basket of supplies upstairs with Jane's help. Vivian emerged after them carrying a list of things to do.

"First we have to set the table with freshly polished silverware and china. Then we need to decorate the room itself. After, we have to fluff the pillows and lay out folded blankets on the sofas. Byron will take care of the rest," Vivian read robotically.

"What about the dress fitting," Jane piped in.

Vivian's tone softened, "That is after we get all of this done, so chop, chop."

Adeline scurried off with Jane, their arms linked. It felt as if they were back at the orphanage again, yet it was different because they weren't frightened anymore.

* * *

After all the work, it was finally time for the dress fitting. Byron had been fit for his tuxedo earlier in the day. Now, only the girls were left. Adeline was to be fitted last. She wondered why she was always last. Was it good or bad?

Adeline stepped into the room. A platform with a long mirror sat in the corner. The rest of the room was filled with dressed mannequins and a man who appeared to be a tailor. Adeline couldn't believe the body shapes of the mannequins. They looked more like dolls than humans, with restricted waists and pointed shoes.

The tailor was a short man with a mustache and smile lines.

"Hello," he said while extending a welcoming hand to Adeline.

Adeline casually walked up to him.

"A nice deep blue would go wonderfully with your hair deary! However, an emerald green would bring out your eyes," the old man debated with himself.

Adeline smirked. This made his smile widen.

"Green it is!" he exclaimed.

Adeline shrugged off her ill-fitting tattered dress and slipped on a soft green ball gown. It was a little big for her, but he quickly pinned it back. The dress had puff sleeves with light green ribbon. It was slightly off the shoulder. The skirt fell to Adeline's mid-calf and exposed her black button up boots. A light green ribbon matching the one on her sleeve was hung in her hair. To finish it off, the tailor clasped a dainty gold heart necklace upon her neck. Adeline felt like royalty.

10

Celebrating Rekindled Relationships

Today was the day of the banquet. Adeline was so excited. Everyone was getting done up in their outfits. Vivian donned a teal dress with pearls. Jane had a purple dress with silver. Byron wore a black jacket and vest with a gold pocket watch. Adeline had on her green dress with gold accents. The tailor had presented their outfits to them prior. He had seemed so happy to see them all done up. Adeline couldn't figure out why the tailor was so happy? Hadn't he just been doing his job? If anything, wouldn't he be embarrassed that he had to work for servants? And on such short notice? No, he was honored, even humbled. Strange.

Miss Smith wore a red, plaid dress with her hair in an updo. Miss Nash had on her signature black and white dress with long gloves. Overall, everyone was in their finest attire. However, that didn't mean that they weren't anxious. They had done their best to set up the party. It was now the job of the guests to decide if they had done their job well.

The table was set and the curtains were drawn. The food was prepared and the guests were arriving. They had put out a buffet earlier so they weren't needed to serve the dinner. It all felt like a dream. This was all too farfetched to be true, but it was true.

Miss Low was already at the door welcoming the guests. Some things never change. Adeline sighed. Even Vivian's mom was dressed up in a gown and chatting with the neighbors. For the first time, everyone at the party was a guest. They were all equal, at least for the night.

Adeline felt lost in the sea of new people and needed an anchor. Adeline walked over to Byron, who was standing by the sofa. Guests were already starting to filter into the dining room for the meal. Byron and Adeline were left alone in the living room with a few other guests.

"This is unreal," Adeline remarked as she sat down next to Byron.

"Yeah," Byron muttered under his breath. "Is something wrong?"

Adeline saw that Byron's eyes were clouded over as if he was in deep thought.

"It's just…this is so great. What do we do after this? We can't work here all of our lives. What will we do? You, you have a voice. You can get a job as a singer or something. I don't. I need something to be good at," Byron said as he looked away.

Byron's eyes looked more at ease now that he had let his feelings overflow. There was still something there though, behind his eyes, and Adeline could see it.

"Come on, Byron," Adeline encourages, "you are good at a lot of things. Like what about all of the odd jobs that you do? And- "

Byron interrupted, "Adeline, anyone can do those things."

"Fine, you have left me with no choice."

Byron gave Adeline a confused look as he asked, "Pardon me, but what-"

They kissed.

She couldn't believe that she had actually done it. Byron hadn't pulled away.

Now Byron stared at Adeline in shock. Both of their faces were flushed. Before things became any more awkward, Adeline got up and went into the other room. Byron needed time to register what just happened. He seemed stunned. To be honest, Adeline was too.

Adeline entered the crowded dining room. Everyone was beginning to sit down. Adeline spotted an empty seat near Jane and walked over. Someone tapped her on the shoulder. She turned but no one was there. She started to chat with Jane when she felt a tap on her shoulder again.

"One moment," she excused herself from Jane.

Maybe it was a guest playing a trick on her? Maybe, it was even Byron? Adeline stood and looked around the room but no one seemed suspicious. Then, she heard a rustle of skirts.

Adeline followed the sound, relying only on her ears. She found an old woman with gray hair. The woman wore a brown dress and shawl with a silver brooch. The tips of the woman's shoes stuck out from under her long dress. The woman smiled when she met Adeline's gaze.

"Sorry," Adeline muttered apologetically. It was just a little old woman minding her own business. Why had Adeline rushed over to her as if she was an intruder of some sort?

Then the woman cleared her throat and spoke in a rusty voice. "Are you Adeline Wickhart?"

FIN.

About the Author

Cassandra Carraher is a student and aspiring author. She is currently in the 8th grade. Her first book, *Adeline*, began as her Girl Scout Silver Award Project and quickly became a passion. She hopes that this book will inspire girls who want to become Girl Scouts or are already Girl Scouts.

"It helps to paint a picture amongst a gallery of paintings. It is the reader's job to choose which painting to study or learn about. This story is all about perspective and experience. Depending on who you are or where you have been, my hope is that you can find a character to relate to. I hope that they look deeper into my painting and see it's hidden meanings," Cassandra says.

Cassandra would like to encourage any young person out there to follow their creative dreams and develop a love for something. "When I was writing

Adeline I couldn't help but write," she says. "There was one time when I came up with an idea in the car and needed to write it down. I pulled up the trusty 'notes' section on my phone. My mother looked at me oddly as I vigorously typed away. That is how *Adeline* originated. Who would have thought that a random idea in the car could have turned into a real story? I know I wasn't expecting it."

Cassandra currently resides in New York with her mother (Jennifer) and father (William) whom she appreciates greatly. Her mother even went as far as starting their own Troop when Cassandra showed interest in Scouting. "My parents helped to shape my world. They gave me opportunities that changed my outlook on life. Without them I would be a completely different person."